It's Just in Time, Amber Brown

PAULA DANZIGER

Illustrated by Tony Ross

SCHOLASTIC INC.

New York Toronto London Auckland Sydney
Mexico City New Delhi Hong Kong Buenos Aires

Thanks to my wonderful consultants—Sheryl Hardin
and her absolutely terrific second-grade class of 1999–2000,
"The Brainy Bunch" from Gullett Elementary School
in Austin, Texas

—*Paula Danziger*

ISBN 0-439-30205-6

Text copyright © 2001 by Paula Danziger
Illustrations copyright © 2001 by Tony Ross.
All rights reserved.
Published by Scholastic Inc., 555 Broadway, New York, NY 10012,
by arrangement with G.P. Putnam's Sons, an imprint of Penguin Putnam Books
for Young Readers, a division of Penguin Putnam Inc.
SCHOLASTIC and associated logos are trademarks and/or
registered trademarks of Scholastic Inc.

12 11 10 9 8 7 6 5 4 3 2 1   2 3 4 5 6 7/0

Printed in the U.S.A.   23

First Scholastic printing, January 2002

Designed by Gunta Alexander
Text set in Calisto

To Marc, Laurie and Eliza (whom I wanted
to be named Amber) Brown —P. D.

I, Amber Brown,

am one very excited six-year,

364-day-old kid.

I am so excited

that I am dancing with my toy gorilla.

He is a two-year,

364-day-old gorilla.

I got him on my fourth birthday.

Tomorrow, July 7, is our birthday.

Last year I was six on July 7.

Next year I will be eight on July 7.

This year I will be seven on July 7.

This is the only day of my life

when my age is the same number

as the day of the month and the month of the year.

Tomorrow will be so special.

It's my birthday *and* my aunt Pam

is here visiting us in New Jersey.

She lives in California.

"Gorilla, I hope someone remembers

that I really want a watch for my birthday."

I, Amber Brown, want a watch

more than anything else in the world.

I, Amber Brown, do not like to keep asking,

"What time is it?" I, Amber Brown, like to know

some things without asking.

That is much more grown-up.

I go downstairs into the kitchen.

Aunt Pam is dyeing my mom's hair.

Actually, she is giving it streaks.

My mom says her hair is

"Boring Sarah Brown brown."

Aunt Pam is putting foil

on some of my mom's hair.

That's how you make streaks,

but it makes my mom look

like a creature in a horror movie.

"Stop fidgeting," Aunt Pam says to Mom.

My mom stops fidgeting.

I think fidgeting runs in our family.

My dad says that I, Amber Brown,

am a major fidget.

I look in the refrigerator for something to eat.

My birthday cake is just sitting there,

waiting for tomorrow.

I scoop up some icing from the bottom of the cake.

My mom, who isn't even looking at me, says,

"Amber Brown. Stay away from that icing."

I lick my finger quickly and try to smooth out

the icing so that it looks even again.

I grab an apple and close the refrigerator.

"Mom. Aunt Pam," I say.

"I think it is a good idea

for me to open one of my presents today."

I, Amber Brown, think that a person should open

one present the night before her birthday

and one on Christmas Eve.

Both of them shake their heads no.

The foil on my mom's head

makes a crinkly sound.

My dad walks into the room.

He looks at my mom's head, laughs, and says,

"Curses. Foiled again."

They just look at him.

The phone rings.

I rush to answer it.

It's my best friend, Justin Daniels.

"I'll be over in three minutes," he says.

"I'll bring the bat and ball."

"Great." I look at the clock

on the wall when we hang up.

One minute. Two minutes.

Three minutes. Four minutes.

I fidget. It's boring standing here,

but I need to know the exact time so

I can tell Justin how late he is.

I, Amber Brown, am trying to help

my best friend be on time

now that we are both almost seven years old.

"Mom," I say. "May I borrow your watch?"

She and Aunt Pam look at each other and smile.

She nods and hands it to me.

I take it and go outside.

Eight minutes. Nine minutes. Ten minutes.

I know that Justin can be at my house

in one minute and forty-two seconds.

I timed it once when I ran to his house.

We live next door to each other.

I keep looking at the watch.

The second hand just keeps moving around.

The minute hand keeps moving . . . very, very slowly.

I look down.

A caterpillar is crawling across my shoe.

It's going faster than Justin must be moving.

Maybe he fell into a hole in the lawn

and was captured by a gang of worms

that want him to do their dirty work for them.

I stare at my mom's watch again.

I know Justin is not an on-time kind of kid,

but lately he just keeps getting later and later.

I want to play ball, but Justin,

the ball, and the bat are not here.

The caterpillar is almost off my shoe.

I wait until it gets off

and then I go back into the kitchen.

Aunt Pam is drying my mom's hair.

Aunt Pam doesn't look very happy.

My mom's hair is a mixture

of Boring Sarah Brown brown

and bright orange streaks.

Now she looks like a cartoon character.

"I'm here." Justin walks into the kitchen.

"Anything good to eat?"

I look at my wrist.

"You said three minutes, Justin.

You said *that* a half hour ago."

He just smiles at me.

"Justin Time," my mom sings.

"I found you just in time."

Grown-ups sing that song a lot to Justin.

"Justin Daniels." I put my hands on my hips.

"You are not 'Justin Time.'

You are Justin Trouble."

Justin just shrugs.

Then he looks at my mom's hair.

"Did you want that color hair?

You look just like a pumpkin."

My mom jumps up and rushes into the bathroom.

"Aaaaaaarg," she yells.

"Justin," I say, "I think that it's time for us
to go out and play ball."

"Watching your mom is fun," Justin says.

"I don't think so," I say.

I look at the watch again.

It's definitely time to get out of here.

I take off the watch and put it on the counter.

Justin and I go outside.

He pitches a ball and I hit it hard.

"Justin," I ask, "why were you so late?"

"I was only a few minutes late," he says.

"Thirty-two and three-quarters minutes,

to be exact."

I, Amber Brown, realize

that it's never going to be easy

to get my friend to care about time.

"Oh, let's just play ball," I say.

"In a minute." Justin very slowly winds up
and starts to pitch in slow motion.

I go over and pull his baseball cap over his eyes.

He pushes the cap up off his eyes.

"I can pitch an alarm clock instead of a ball.

Then you can watch time fly," I say, laughing.

"You know what they call a dog

that can tell time?" Justin asks.

I just stare at him.

"A watch dog!" He laughs.

It's hard to stay annoyed at Justin.

I guess we just feel differently about some things.

"And you know what they call a boy

who doesn't worry about what time it is?"

He just smiles at me.

"Not 'Justin Time'. . . but Justin Daniels,"

I, Amber Brown, say, grinning.

"And you know what they call

the best friend of the boy

who doesn't worry about time?

. . . Amber Brown."

My mom calls out,

"Lunchtime. Justin, your mom says

that you can eat with Amber."

We rush inside.

My mom is standing there

with a scarf on her head.

"Aunt Pam and I are going to the salon

to get this fixed."

Aunt Pam shakes her head.

"I don't understand. I followed instructions."

My dad is in the kitchen.

"I'm in charge of lunch."

"Yea! Pizza! But hold the anchovies,"

Justin and I yell at the same time.

This is a wonderful day-before-my-birthday day.

"Happy birthday, Mr. Gorilla," I say

when I wake up the next morning.

Mr. Gorilla says, "Happy birthday, Amber."

Actually, I am just pretending, but it feels real.

I, Amber Brown, am seven years old.

My party isn't until four o'clock.

All morning I try not to think about my presents

even though I want to know what they are.

Finally, it's almost time for my party.

I try on the new clothes that Aunt Pam brought
all the way from California.

I look out the window and see my mom and dad,
Aunt Pam, Mr. and Mrs. Daniels, and Danny.

Even Justin is there—on time.

I say to Gorilla,

"Cross your fingers that I get a watch."

Gorilla just sits there.

I rush downstairs

and outside to my birthday barbecue.

"Don't you look pretty?" Mrs. Daniels says.

Justin stands behind her making faces at me.

I make a face back.

Lunch . . . it's wonderful!

Justin and I make hot dogs

with catsup and marshmallows on top.

Mom brings out the cake.

Danny wants to blow out the candles, too.

Today I am seven years old.

I am much more grown-up,

so I let Danny blow out the candles with me.

When we finish, I say, "I want cake from the side
that Danny did not spit on."

Everyone except Danny eats cake from that side.

I think that on Danny's next birthday,
his mom should just put spit icing on the cake.

"Now it's time for the presents," Dad says.

He puts them on the table.

Danny hands me a present.

Even without unwrapping it, I can tell it's a bat.

Danny asks to open a present and I let him,

just as long as he remembers it is mine.

Aunt Pam hands me a present.

"I thought the clothes were my present," I say.

"This, too." She smiles.

I open it. It's a pig alarm clock.

I pretend that it's a watch.

I listen to the pig oink.

I turn to let Justin look at it up close.

He's not there.

Before I can ask where he is,

my dad hands me a present.

"I think it's about TIME for this."

I, Amber Brown, think I know what it is.

It's definitely not a ball to go with the bat.

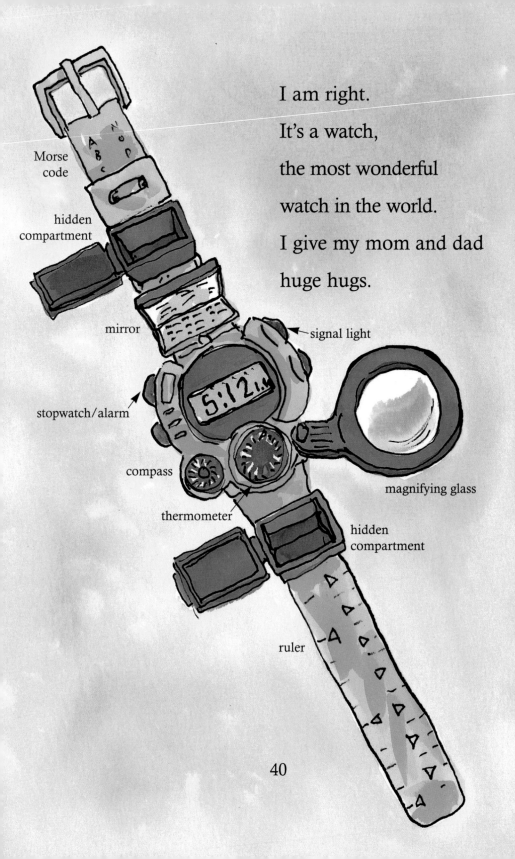

I am right.
It's a watch,
the most wonderful
watch in the world.
I give my mom and dad
huge hugs.

Morse code

hidden compartment

mirror

signal light

stopwatch/alarm

compass

thermometer

magnifying glass

hidden compartment

ruler

40

Then Mr. Daniels says,

"Someone asked me to give this to you."

I rip the badly wrapped present open.

It's one part of a walkie-talkie.

"Here's the card that goes with it."

Mr. Daniels hands it to me.

Roses are red
Vilets are blue
with this Walkie-talkie
I can have a good time
with you!!!

Justin

"Justin made the card for you yesterday,"

his mom says.

"He wouldn't even let me help him with the spelling."

I hear a "BOO" from my walkie-talkie.

Then I hear Justin's voice. "That's why I was late."

I look at the walkie-talkie, grin, and talk into it.

"Thank you . . . where are you?"

"You're welcome," Justin says. "Come and find me.
I'll give you clues over the walkie-talkie."

I push a button on the side of my watch
to time how long it will take me to find him.

I, Amber Brown, have learned something
very important on my birthday.
My best friend is on Justin Time . . .
and that works for him.
And I, Amber Brown, am on Amber Brown Time . . .
and that works for me.

Look out, world . . .

it's time for both of us.